MONSTERS 101®

"Late Enrollment"

by M. RASHEED

A
Second Sight Graphix
Publication
7413 Six Forks Rd, Suite #203
Raleigh, NC 27615
http://www.mrasheed.com

Monsters 101, Book Four
"Late Enrollment"

Story & Art
by

M. RASHEED

ISBN: 978-0-578-056364

Library of Congress Control Number: 2010901715

First published in 2010
Second Sight Graphix
7413 Six Forks Rd, Suite #203
Raleigh, NC 27615
http://www.mrasheed.com

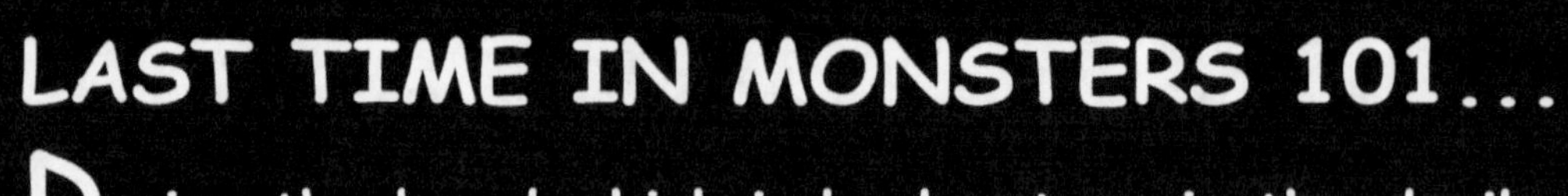

During the boys' whirlwind adventure in the devil world of Dharokalee, Mort is hailed as a hero for returning the magick fork that got them there. As his reward, he is instructed in wonderful secrets and ancient lore by the High Magician Pherlyren! But now that they are returning home, will Mort get to find the secret order of super magicians Pherlyren said would train him before he's devoured by an old foe?

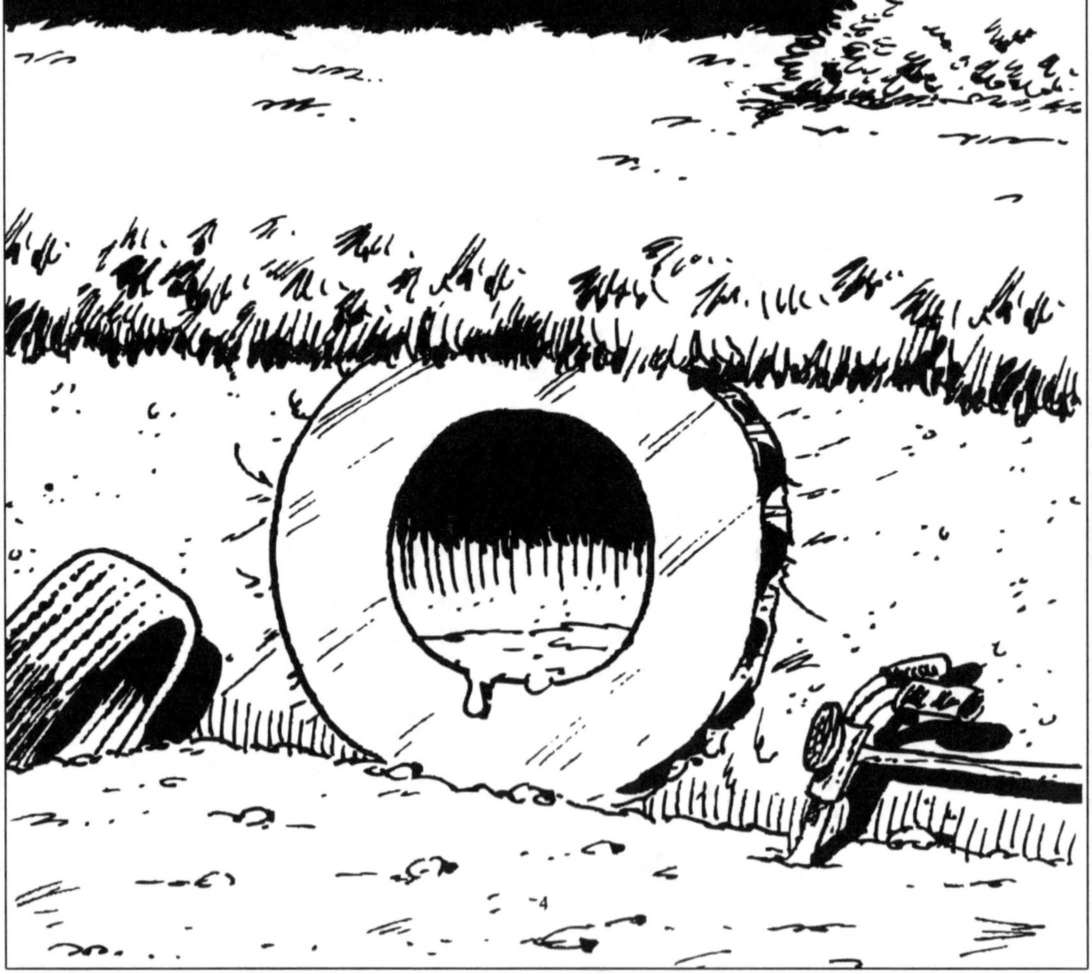

VERY PECULIAR FACES YOU WEAR IN THIS SACRED PLACE!
AYE. I HOPE FOR YOUR SAKES THERE IS A **GOOD** REASON FOR THE PRESENCE OF A NASHERAN!

SHUT UP AND GET OUT OF OUR WAY.

BOLD TALK! THERE'S **NOTHING** FOR YOU HERE. GO BACK TO THAT TOILET YOU CALL A HOME OR THERE'LL BE TROUBLE!

MY JOB IS TO SPLIT THE SKULLS OF **AUK!!**

HOY THERE! WHY **YOU**--!
SLASH!
5

THUD!
CHOMP!

BLORCH!

SHAKT!!
UNH!

IT MUST SUCK TO GET YOUR BUTT KICKED BY LOWLY NASHERANS.
YOU THINK? SNRK
PIPE IT!
LET'S GO.

6

YOU QUEST FOR THE GREAT AXE?
STEP FORWARD.

WHAT, DO I HAVE TO FIGHT **YOU?** LET'S DO IT THEN!

YOU SEEK DRAGON'S FANG, THE MAGICK LEGENDARY WEAPON OF SHARGAYT, THE SEAWOLF OF RED PLAIN SHEE.
YUP.

HE SEAWOLF WAS THE GREATEST HERO IN FAERIE HISTORY. HIS MAGICK AXE HELPED MAKE THAT POSSIBLE.

SINCE SEAWOLF'S DEATH, DRAGON'S FANG HAS FALLEN INTO THE HANDS OF **MANY**...
...THOUGH **FEW** OF THEM WERE OF SHARGAYT'S AWESOME HEROIC STATURE, AND USED THE POWER TO CAUSE STRIFE AND GRIEF IN THE LAND.

HE COLLECTIVE ONARCHS OF HE SHEES ECREED THAT RAGON'S FANG ILL NO LONGER E PASSED ALONG ROM WRETCH O WRETCH...

...BUT ONLY THE MOST **UPRIGHT** AND **HEROIC** PROSPECTS WILL BE ALLOWED TO CLAIM IT.
BE **YOU** SUCH A BEING?

OH, ABSOLUTELY.
7

THEN HEAR THIS:
A TALE OF SHARGAYT HIMSELF AS TOLD BY NONE OTHER THAN ME.

I DIDN'T COME HERE FOR NO STORIES, CHIEF.

IT IS THE WAY IT IS ALWAYS DONE.

IF YOU DON'T HEAR THE TALE THEN YOU DON'T QUE--!
OH, ALRIGHT!! GO AHEAD!!

THEN ATTEND.
HEAR AS I UNFOLD AN ADVENTURE FOUND WITHIN THE LONG LIFE OF SHARGAYT THE SEAWOLF.
8

WHAT'S THIS? I DID NOT ASK FOR MORE WINE.

ACCEPT THIS SMALL OFFERING ON BEHALF OF THIS LOWLY SERVANT, I BEG OF YOU, MY LORD.

THE PATRONS ARE ON THEIR BEST BEHAVIOR WHEN YOU ARE AMONG US, AND I FOR ONE, AM GRATEFUL.

IN THAT CASE, I ACCEPT. WITH THANKS.
HOW VERY BIG OF YOU.

EH?
PROBLEMS, GENTLEMEN?
YAH! 'TIS YOU!

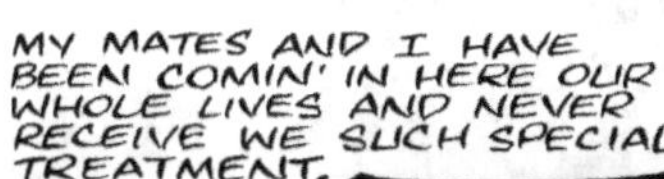
MY MATES AND I HAVE BEEN COMIN' IN HERE OUR WHOLE LIVES AND NEVER RECEIVE WE SUCH SPECIAL TREATMENT.

NOT FAIR IT IS.
Y'DAMN RIGHT.
9

IS IT TRUE WHAT THEY SAY? YOU'RE AN IMMORTAL WHO'LL RISE TO HEAVEN WHEN HE TIRES OF THE EARTH?

"A FIST FULL OF LEGEND"
STORY AND ART BY M. RASHEED © 2010
KILLED ONE DAY I MAY BE...
...BUT NOT BY YOU LOT.
11

P-PUT THEM DOWN!

YOU MAY HAVE THEM!
AND GLADLY!

UNGH!
OOF!
DUNH!

TAKE THE HINT, GENTLEMEN. I ONLY WISH TO ENJOY MY DRINK.

I'D HATE TO HAVE TO TAKE THIS SCUFFLE TO ITS ULTIMATE CONCLUSION SHOULD YOU INSIST ON BEING STUBBORN!
AYE!
THAT I AM, SEA DOG!

I'LL NOT SEE THE LIKES OF FAERIE SCUM SUCKING DOWN WHAT SHOULD RIGHTLY BE MINE!
12

TWAK!

UHHH...!

BUH!
GAK!
NNHF!

THIS TAVERN IS A PLACE OF PEACE, GENTLEMEN.
YOU THREE ARE NO LONGER WELCOME.

I'D BETTER NOT HEAR OF--!
EH?
SEAWOLF!
SEAWOLF IT REALLY IS YOU!

WHAT IS IT, LAD?
A GREAT BEAST RAVAGES MY VILLAGE! PLEASE! YOU MUST HELP!
13

SPEAK, MAN! WHAT IS IT?
I- I DON'T KNOW!
IT CAME FROM BEYOND!

"IT ATTACKED THE WOMENFOLK FIRST! EVEN NOW THEY LIE HELPLESS ON THEIR PALLETS!"
"NOTHING WAKES THEM!"

"THE MEN ARE SLAVES TO THE CREATURE, SERVING IT MINDLESSLY!"

ONLY I MANAGED TO ESCAPE.
HOW FAR?

WE CAN BE THERE BY SUNDOWN!
I WILL LEAD THE WAY!

THEN LET US SET OFF.
I HAVE AN IDEA OF WHAT PLAGUES YOUR PEOPLE.
IF THE MAKER BE WITH US, YOU'LL BE FREE OF THE BEAST BY MORN!
THANK YOU, SEA WOLF! THANK YOU!
14

SEAWOLF, IS IT TRUE THAT YOUR FATHER IS A HALF ANGEL?
YES. HE IS A SPRITE.

AND IS IT TRUE THAT YOU SLEW TEN THOUSAND GIANTS TO CAPTURE DRAGON'S FANG FROM THE SORCEROR SLEVIN OF KARNORA?

HA!
NO, I CARVED MY AXE MYSELF FROM THE SKULL OF A DRAGON KILLED IN MY FIRST BATTLE.
I BECAME A MAN THAT DAY.

ENOUGH OF ME. WHAT OF YOU?
ME?
YES.
WHAT OF YOUR ACCOMPLISH-MENTS?

WELL, JUST THIS MONTH I FILLED MY GRAIN COFFER TO THE POWER MARK.
ON THE SOLSTICE EVE THE ELDERS WILL CHOOSE MY BRIDE!
15

YOU MUST BE VERY EXCITED.
OH, I AM!

I AM THE LAST OF MY PEERS TO START A FAMILY.

MY FRIENDS TEASED ME MERCILESSLY OVER IT, BUT NOW IT IS OVER.

I'M LOOKING FORWARD TO LIFE AS A WHOLE MAN, BUT ADMIT TO A CERTAIN AMOUNT OF CONCERN AS TO WHAT TO EXPECT FROM THE WEDDING NIGHT.

HA HA! YOU HAVE LITTLE TO FEAR, YOUNG TALEN. TRUST THAT SINCE MAN/WOMAN RELATIONS HAVE PERFORMED SMOOTHLY FOR ALL OF THESE AEONS...

...THERE'S NO REASON TO BELIEVE THAT THE SYSTEM WILL SUDDENLY FAIL JUST BECAUSE YOU ARE NOW INVOLVED IN IT. I'M SURE YOU WILL MAKE A FINE HUSBAND.
THANK YOU.

16

...AND IS IT TRUE WHAT THEY SAY ABOUT THE--?
ENOUGH.
TRULY I GROW WEARY OF THIS RELENTLESS INTERROGATION.

TELL ME MORE ABOUT THIS BEAST.
EH?

I THOUGHT YOU SAID YOU ALREADY HAD AN IDEA OF WHAT IT WAS?

I DO.
BASED ON THE INFO I WAS GIVEN. IT'S POSSIBLE SOMETHING WAS LEFT OUT IN YOUR EXCITEMENT.

TELL ME MORE. WHAT IS IT LIKE?
OH, IT IS TERRIBLE!
VICIOUS!
WORSE THAN ANY OTHER VILE CREATURE YOU HAVE FACED, I AM SURE!

NO DOUBT IT WILL TAX ALL OF YOUR CONSIDERABLE ABILITY TO SUBDUE IT.
AND WHY DO YOU THINK IT HAS CHOSEN YOUR VILLAGE AS ITS LAIR?
17

BAH!
WHO KNOWS WHY THESE ABOMINATIONS CHOOSE THE PATHS THEY FOLLOW?
WHY THE QUESTIONS ALL OF A SUDDEN? THE GREAT SEAWOLF ISN'T DEVELOPING A COWARDLY STREAK?
HARDLY.
I'M ONLY LOOKING FOR ANYTHING TO GIVE ME AN EDGE IN THE COMING BATTLE.

I MUST SAY I AM QUITE DISAPPOINTED. YOU ARE VERY DIFFERENT THAN YOUR REPUTATION. A TRUE WARRIOR, IN MY OPINION, SHOULD JUMP FEET FIRST INTO DANGER AND SHOW THE HEART FOR GLORY.

IN MY EXPERIENCE, THE WARRIORS WITH THAT ATTITUDE RARELY SURVIVED THEIR FIRST BATTLE.

WHATEVER STATION IN LIFE ONE SEEKS TO PURSUE, IT SHOULD BE DONE WITH SUCCESS IN MIND.
18

IT'S VERY QUIET.

HOY!!

DO YOU SEE?

THEIR MINDS ARE NOT THEIR OWN.

HEY MOVE AS IF SOME OTHER FORCE TUGS THEM ALONG.

HERE, SEAWOLF!
IT IS TO HERE THEY ARE DRAWN!
19

THIS IS THE GREAT BEAST THAT PLAGUES MY PEOPLE!!
AS I SUSPECTED! A GREEN DAUGHTER!

A WHAT?!
AN AVATAR OF THE MOTHER GODDESS! A PARASITIC SPIRIT THAT ACCEPTS WORSHIP ON HER BEHALF!

SHE WILL STAY AND CONSUME ALL OF YOUR RESOURCES UNTIL THE PEOPLE STARVE TO DEATH IN DEVOTED ADORATION!

NO!!
WAIT! THERE'S NOTHING YOU CAN DO!

YOU'RE WRONG! CAN'T YOU SEE?! I'M SPECIAL! I'M THE ONLY MALE WHO CAN RESIST ITS POWER!

IT IS MY DESTINY TO STOP THE BEAST!

ARROooo?
LEAVE US BE!!

GAH!!

AAAAAAA!
21

RAAH!
RELEASE HIM!

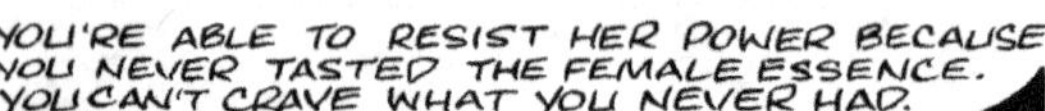
YOU'RE ABLE TO RESIST HER POWER BECAUSE YOU NEVER TASTED THE FEMALE ESSENCE. YOU CAN'T CRAVE WHAT YOU NEVER HAD.

LEAVE THIS TO THE ONE WHOSE EXPERTISE YOU SOUGHT.
YOU ARE RIGHT.

ROAR!!
HOLD, **BEAST**!
NO VIRGIN PEASANT FARMER DO YOU FIND IN **ME**! I AM YOUR VANQUISHER! AND MY MAGIC AXE YOUR WOE!

PROOF IT IS AGAINST YOUR POWER!
WAM!

ITS BITE THE SKURGE OF ALL THOSE WHO TROUBLE THE INNOCENT!
22

"AS AN IMMORTAL SPIRIT, THE GREEN DAUGHTER COULD NOT BE DESTROYED, BUT SEAWOLF WAS ABLE TO CAUSE HER SUCH DISTRESS, THAT SHE WITHDREW TO THE COLD VOID BEYOND FROM WHENCE SHE CAME!"

"WITH HER GONE, HER SPELL OVER THE VILLAGERS WAS FINALLY BROKEN..."

"...AND YOUNG TALEN WAS CELEBRATED AS A HERO, AND LIVED THE REST OF HIS DAYS IN COMFORT."

SUCH IS THE TALE OF SEAWOLF!

OH, IS IT OVER?

ARE YOU READY TO TEST YOUR HEROIC METTLE?
HECK YEAH!
ARE YOU KIDDING?
23

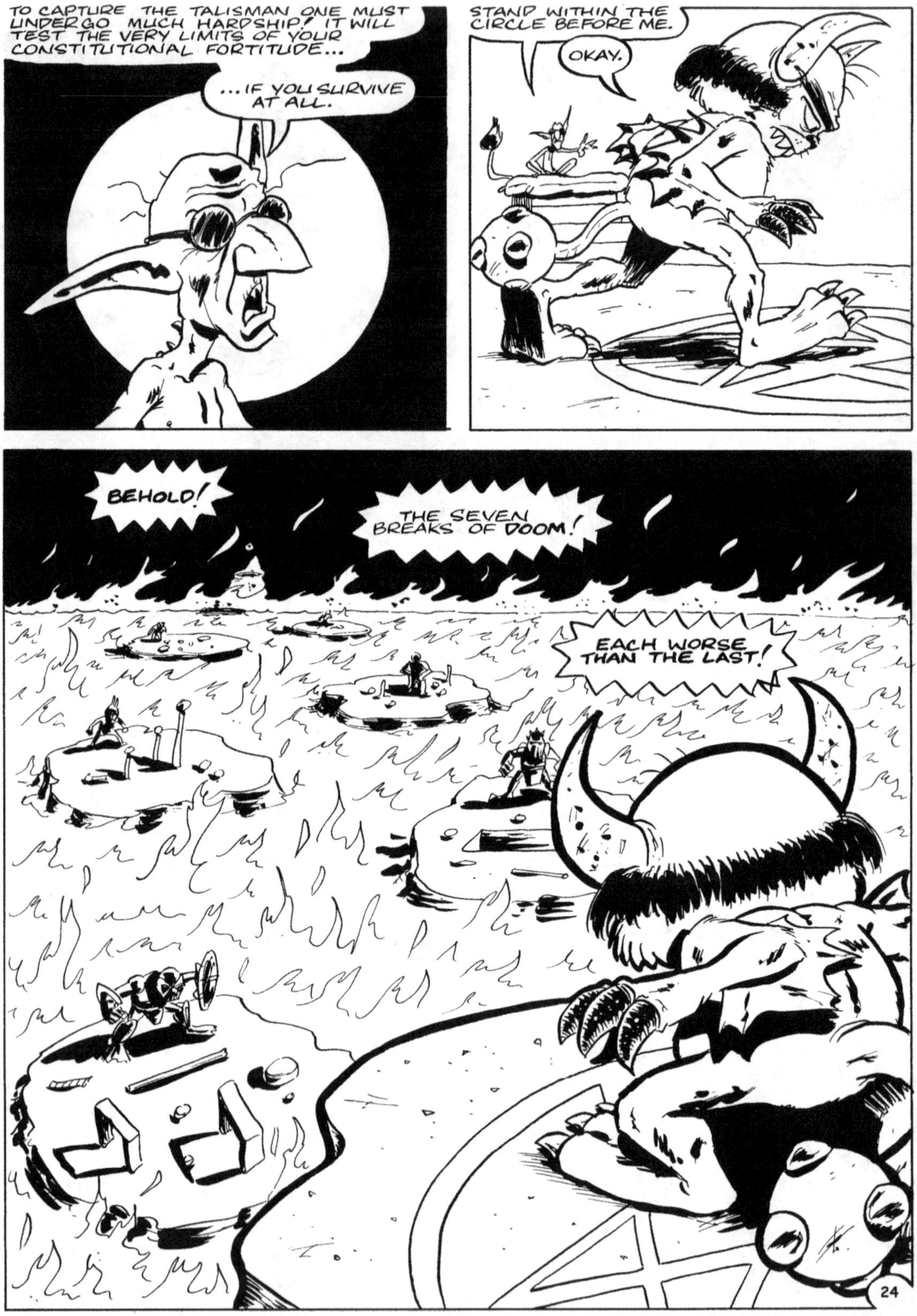

BEHOLD!

THE SEVEN BREAKS OF **DOOM**!

EACH WORSE THAN THE LAST!

24

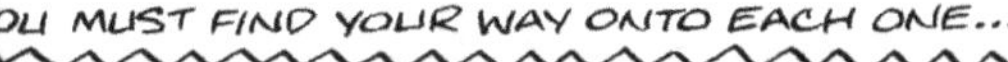
OU MUST FIND YOUR WAY ONTO EACH ONE...

...CORRECTLY SOLVE EACH PUZZLE...

...THEN CONQUER EACH GUARDIAN!
ONLY THEN CAN YOU OBTAIN DRAGON'S FANG!

WAIT...!
WHAT IS THIS?!

GRAB!!

DO YOU LIKE APPLES?
PARDON?
NOTHIN'!
25

YOU DID IT, MAESCUS!
AM I THE MAN OR WHAT?

MOST IMPRESSIVE. OF THE 1,970 BEINGS WHO HAVE SOUGHT THE AXE, YOU ARE ONE OF THE SIX TO HAVE SURVIVED THE QUEST...

...AND ONE OF THE TWO BEINGS TO ACTUALLY WIN DRAGON'S FANG.
HA!

AND HE DIDN'T DO IT AS QUICKLY.
SWEETNESS.
NOW HOW DO I TURN IT ON?

TO ACTIVATE THE OWNERSHIP SPELL OF DRAGON'S FANG, YOU MUST WHISPER ITS TRUE NAME INTO THE POMMEL.
WELL, WHAT'S THE NAME?

THE NAME CAN ONLY BE WON BY ENTERING THAT DOOR AND FACING THE MANIFESTED REALITY OF YOUR GREATEST FEAR.
WHAT?!
NEXT:
"NO PLACE LIKE HOME"

YOU MUST FACE THE MANIFESTED REALITY OF YOUR GREATEST FEAR ON THE OTHER SIDE OF THIS DOOR. ONLY THEN WILL THE POWER OF DRAGON'S FANG BE YOURS.
YOU MUST BE JOKING!

YOU PUT ME THROUGH ALL OF THAT TO GET THE THING, NOW YOU'RE GIVING ME THE RUNAROUND JUST TO TURN IT ON?!

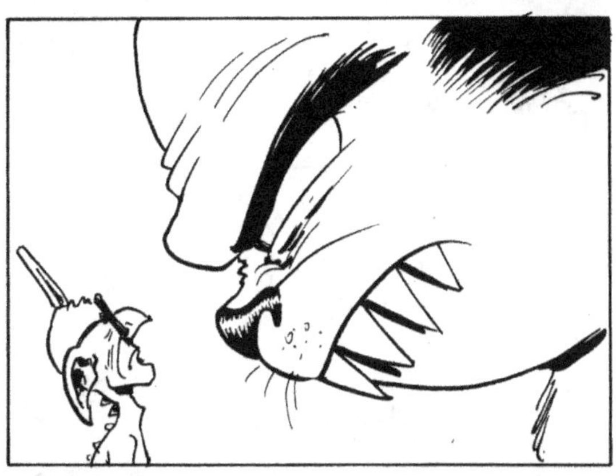

I WOULD BUST YOUR HEAD IF I DIDN'T SUSPECT YOUR BLIND-GIMP SCHTICK TO BE A SHAM.
YOU ARE WISER THAN YOUR STENCH WOULD INDICATE.

I AM PRENT LIGGEN, GUARDIAN OF THE FIRE LANDS. I WAS CHARGED TO MAKE SURE THAT ONLY THOSE WHO PASSED THE TEST CLAIM THE AXE'S POWER, AND I CERTAINLY HAVE THE MIGHT TO ENFORCE THE EDICT.
29

WILL YOU BE CONTINUING?
YES, DANG IT!

BUT THESE TWO ARE GOING WITH ME.
VERY WELL. GO ON THROUGH THE DOOR WHEN YOU ARE READY.

SOMETHING TELLS ME YOU PEOPLE REALLY DON'T WANT ANYONE TO GET THE AXE ANYWAY.

IT IS A FAERIE WEAPON. YOU ARE NOT FAERIE. NEED I SAY MORE?

JERK.

WHAT DID HE MEAN BY THAT, MAESCUS?

IT MEANS THE TESTS ARE EASIER IF YOU ARE ONE OF THEM.
30

WHAT DO YOU FEAR, SEEKERS OF THE NAME? WHAT DO YOU FEAR, FOR THAT IS WHAT YOU MUST FACE...

NOW. WOULDN'T IT SUCK TO HAVE TO FIGHT A PISSED OFF ZOMBIE OF THAT SEAWOLF GUY?

WHAT?

DID I ERR?!
LODETH, I HOPE THIS THING KILLS YOU FIRST.
31

MAESCUS, I SWEAR, I DIDN'T MEAN--!
SHUT UP AND GET OVER THERE.

HSS!!

KEEP AN EYE OUT FOR A WEAKNESS WE CAN EXPLOIT.
RIGHT.

BAM!

YOU'RE ON YOUR OWN, BOSS
OH, NO YOU DON'T!

YOU HIT 'EM LOW, I'LL HIT 'EM HIGH.
SNRK

YAAAH!!

CLUMP
THUD!

WAK!
WAK!

WH-WHAT DID HE SAY?
I DON'T KNOW... SOMETHING IN HIS ANCIENT LANGUAGE FROM WAY BACK WHEN.

HE'S BLAMING IT ON **US**, WHATEVER IT IS.

AWWW, HERE HE COMES!!
LOOK OUT!

WHOOMP!
33

SLASH!

OOF!!

WHAT ARE WE GOING TO DO, BOSS?
I'M THINKING...

"MANIFESTED REALITY?"

YOU KNOW... I THINK THIS REALLY IS A ZOMBIE OF SEAWOLF! THIS IS REALLY THE GUY!
34

WHAT?
LOOK AT HIM. HE'S BEEN DEAD FOR A ZILLION YEARS. HE'S CONFUSED AND DISORIENTED...

THEY ACTUALLY BROUGHT THE REAL GUY BACK TO LIFE!

BUT HOW CAN YOU BE SURE?

THERE'S ONLY ONE WAY TO KNOW.

HEY, BUD.
I HAVE YOUR AXE.
WANT IT?

BINGO.
35

THAT'S IT...
C'MON.

A LITTLE MORE.

...AND OFF YA GO!
BOOT!

IT'S MINE!!
I KNOW THE NAME!!

IT'S OVER!! LET US IN BEFORE HE COMES BACK ALL SCARY AND ON FIRE!!
36

OU MUST BE VERY PLEASED
ITH YOURSELF.
WHAT DO **YOU** THINK?

I THINK YOU SHOULD LISTEN TO THIS INSTRUCTION AND GO.

THE NAME IS A MAGIC SPELL IN ITS OWN RIGHT. EVEN NOW YOU SHOULD FEEL IT STRUGGLING TO ESCAPE YOUR THICK, BRUTISH HEAD.
IT'S **KILLING** YOU, ISN'T IT?

NCE UTTERED IT
ILL ESCAPE AND
ANISH FROM YOUR
MIND.
WHISPER IT INTO THE POMMEL AND THE POWER IS YOURS.

AND IT WILL REMAIN SO FOR AS LONG AS THE WEAPON IS IN YOUR POSSESSION.

F YOU WALK AWAY FROM IT, IT **WILL** RETURN
O ITS DORMANT STATE, AND YOU WILL
HAVE TO FACE YOUR FEAR TO ACTIVATE
T AGAIN.
THAT IS ALL.
NOW **GO!!**
37

"NO PLACE LIKE HOME"
STORY AND ART BY M. RASHEED © 2010

AH!! SMELL THAT AIR!
COOL!
HE SENT US BACK TO THE CAVE!

I WAS AFRAID WE'D END UP IN NEPAL OR SOMETHING.
BYE BYE, FELLAS! NO HARD FEELIN'S!
WAIT, BENKOM!

I WANT TO TEST THIS SPELL ON YOU.
W-WHAT!

HEY, NO!! I THOUGHT WE HAD A TRUCE!

I'M RESTORED!!
HOW'D YOU DO THAT?!
A LITTLE BIRDIE TAUGHT ME.

GREAT! I HATE OWING FOLKS! LOOK ME UP IF YOU NEED ME!
OKAY! STAY OUT OF TROUBLE!
YEAH, RIGHT!
39

WAP!

WHATCHU DO THAT FOR? YOU SHOULDA LET THAT GUY **ROT**! DIDN'T HE TRY TO KILL US 80 TIMES?

AWW, DON'T BE LIKE THAT, PUGROFF. I NEEDED TO TEST THAT SPELL OUT ON **SOMEBODY**.
I ♡ π

PLUS IT WON'T HURT YOU TO ACTUALLY ACT LIKE A GOOD GUY FOR A CHANGE--!
OOP.

HEY..!
WHAT'S THAT?

IT'S THE **FORK**!
Y-YEAH?
SO?

YOU STOLE THE FORK FROM THOSE PEOPLE!!
I DIDN'T **STEAL** IT!!
40

OH, WELL WHAT DO YOU CALL IT THEN?
I-I WAS GOING TO GIVE IT BACK.

I JUST WANTED TO FIGURE OUT HOW IT WORKED!

YOU THINK I...
...ME...
...DON'T KNOW STEALING WHEN I SEE IT?

I DIDN'T STEAL IT!!!
PLUS YOU'RE SWEATING LIKE A DAMN PIG!

PIGS DON'T SWEAT--!
HUH?!

I'LL RELIEVE YOU OF THAT, THANK YOU.

WHAT?
WHAT'S GOING ON?
41

WHO ARE YOU?!

I'M THE ONE WHO MADE THIS.

TCH-- TCHAGIL?
MY FORK OF THE FARWAYS DOESN'T BELONG TO YOU, MORT.

MY PEOPLE ARE VERY IMPRESSED WITH YOU.
I'M RETURNING IT TO SAVE YOUR LEGACY.
YOU MAY THANK ME.

THANK YOU, SIR.
I WOULD THINK THAT A MAGICIAN OF YOUR TALENTS WOULD BE SEEKING TO CREATE HIS OWN TALISMANS...
...NOT STEALING SOMEONE ELSES.

IN THE FUTURE, I EXPECT TO HEAR ONLY GOOD THINGS ABOUT YOU. DO YOU UNDERSTAND ME?
YES, SIR.
42

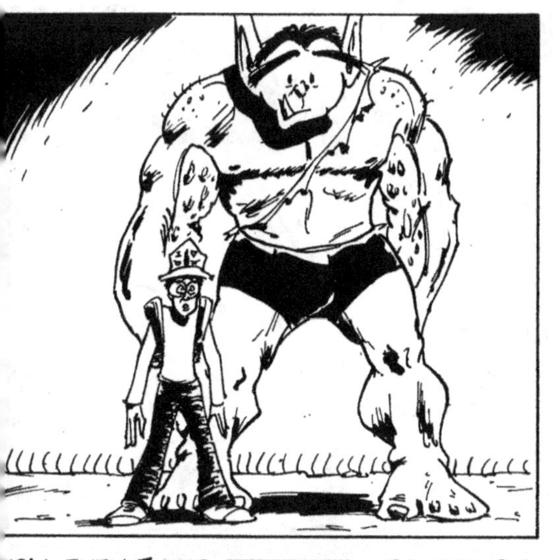

WOW. EVEN I WAS IMPRESSED BY THAT.
HEY.

SO THE BIG, BAD HERO TURNED OUT TO BE A HUMAN AFTER ALL, HUH?
YEAH...

I'M GOING HOME NOW, PUGG. I NEED TO SEE MY GRA'MA.
YOU GOING TO SEE YOUR DAD?

UH... YEAH.
LATER.

I GOTTA GET A HERO BAR IN ME BEFORE I GO NUCLEAR.

OKAY. SEE YOU.
SEE YA.

Z

DAD.
HUNH--?
WHUZ?
USMC

DAD, IT'S ME.
BOY?!
WILLY!
WHERE THE DEVIL HAVE YOU BEEN?!

I THOUGHT YOU WERE DEAD!!

GET IN HERE AND CLEAN THIS PLACE UP.

NAH.
I WON'T BE GOING IN THERE AGAIN.

WHAT?! OH, YOU THINK YOU'RE A **MAN** NOW?!
HUH?!
USMC
NO, DAD.
I'M **NOT** A MAN...

...I'M A MONSTER.

WHA--?

GASP!

IT'S **YOU**!!
WHA--?
WILLY?!
WILLY YOU...
...YOU KILLED THOSE KIDS?!

NO.
NO, I **DIDN'T**.

A-ALRIGHT.
ALRIGHT.
45

I'M GONE, DAD. I WON'T BE BACK.

WELL, WHERE YOU GOIN'?
USMC

I'LL BE OKAY. YOU DON'T HAVE TO WORRY ABOUT ME.
WILLY?!

WILLY?!

WILLY!!!

46

THIS IS MARA PAPAS WITH A CHANNEL SEVEN NEWS LATE-BREAKING SPECIAL REPORT!

A LOCAL SIMLINE BOY LAST SEEN IN THE COMPANY OF THE NOTORIOUS CREATURE SUSPECTED BY POLICE OF BEING INVOLVED IN LAST YEAR'S TANGLEWOOD CHILD MASSACRE, HAS RETURNED TO HIS FAMILY SAFE AND SOUND.

YOUNG MORTISE TENNON WAS REPORTED MISSING FROM HIS HOME LAST SPRING AND LATER SPOTTED BY WITNESSES, INCLUDING SIMLINE POLICE, IN COMPANY WITH A LARGE, WHITE CREATURE DURING ITS FAMOUS BATTLE WITH U.K. SUPERHERO RED SHIELD!

ACCORDING TO POLICE SOURCES, THE BOY DID NOT SEEM TO BE THREATENED BY THE CREATURE, NOR IN ANY KIND OF DANGER FROM IT DURING THE INCIDENT, BUT IN FACT SEEMED TO BE UNDER ITS PROCTETION!

"AMIDST MUCH REJOICING, MORTISE'S GRANDMOTHER, MRS. PATIENCE WHITE, HAD THIS TO SAY:"
OH, THANK YOU, LORD!! THANK YOU FOR BRINGING HIM BACK TO ME!!
...JUST GLAD MY BABY'S HOME!

MORT DON'T YOU EVER SCARE ME LIKE THAT AGAIN! DO YOU HEAR ME?
YES, MA'AM.
DO YOU HEAR ME?
YES. MA'AM!
47

MRS. WHITE, HERSELF HAVING AN EXTENSIVE RECORD OF RUN-INS WITH THE POLICE FROM MILITANT, BLACK NATIONALIST ACTIVITIES DURING THE 1970s IS THE BOY'S SOLE GUARDIAN AND PARENTAL FIGURE!

78496-4328

HEY.
OH, HEY!
THERE YOU ARE.
I THOUGHT YOU'D BE IN THERE ALREADY.

HANKS FOR WHAT YOU SAID.
NO PROBLEM. WE'RE BUDS NOW, RIGHT?
YEAH.

I'M GOING TO NEED YOU TO SCARE THE MESS OUT OF SOMEONE FOR ME.

WHO? YOUR GRANDMA?
HA!
NO, MY COUSIN. I NEED HIM THE HECK **OFF** MY BACK.

MY GRANDMA MOVED HIM IN SO HE COULD WATCH MY EVERY SINGLE, TINY MOVE.*
THESE EVENTS TOOK PLACE IN THE SHORT STORY "THICKER THAN WATER." ~M.R.

IT MADE IT A LOT HARDER TO SNEAK OUT TONIGHT.
49

I SEE.
SCARE THE COUSIN...
...THEN YOUR GRANDMA.
ACTUALLY, I THINK SHE CAN TAKE YOU.
NEXT

"NASHERA"

STORY AND ART BY M. RASHEED © 2010

TIGHTEN IT, BOYS.
ERGH!!

YEAH! YOU THOUGHT YOU WERE ALL OF THAT AND A BAG OF CHIPS, DIDN'T YOU?
DIDN'T YOU?!

HEY!!!
WHAT THE--?!

BENKOM?
Y'KNOW, I MADE A LITTLE PROMISE TO MYSELF FIFTY YEARS AGO WHEN YOU DOUBLE-CROSSED ME AND LEFT ME FOR DEAD IN AN ALIEN WORLD.

WELL, WELL,
WELL.
IF IT AIN'T EVERYONE'S FAVORITE MAGICK FLINGIN' NASHERAN.

I CAN'T WAIT TO--!
SAVE IT, ARSE WIPE.
IF YOU'RE FEELIN' FROGGY THEN JUMP!
54

BENKOM UTTERS BURKERITT'S STREAM OF PULVERIZING LIGHT, HIS MOST POTENT (AND ONLY) OFFENSIVE SPELL...

...BUT DRAGON'S FANG ABSORBS AND DISSIPATES ALL ENERGY HARMLESSLY INTO THE AIR, RENDERING THE SPELL VOID.

THE AXE'S POWER WILL NOT BE DENIED!
ADDING X100 THE FORCE TO EACH CONSECUTIVE SWING!

BLAM!

THWAK!

BRAKKA!
55

THINKING MAESCUS UNATTENTIVE, MORT TRIES AN OFFENSE OF HIS OWN...

...BUT DRAGON'S FANG CANNOT BE TAKE
UNAWARE IN A MAGICK ATTACK!

HEY!!

TINK! TINK!
GET HIM OUT OF THERE!
NO!

DO IT OR I'LL CUT PUGG'S HEAD OFF!
DON'T LISTEN TO HIM, MORT!

"MORT?"
WHY DO I KNOW THAT NAME?

WAIT! MORT! YEAH, THAT'S THE KID YOU USED TO SMACK ALL THE TIME!

WHEN DID YOU LEARN ALL THIS MAGICK STUFF?
A WHOLE LOT HAS HAPPENED SINCE LAST WE SAW YOU.

NO FOOLIN'?
PUGG WHAT ARE YOU PALLING AROUND WITH THIS NERD KID FOR?

HE'S MY...
...FRIEND.

"FRIEND?" FRIEND?!? YOU'RE A MONSTER NOW! HUMAN KIDS AREN'T YOUR FRIENDS! THEY'RE SANDWICHES!

WOW. I TURN YOU INTO A MONSTER AND YOU BECOME SOFT AS CAKE! I GUESS IT'S MY FAULT FOR NOT TRAINING YOU OR SOMETHING.
57

AH, WELL. NOTHING I CAN DO ABOUT IT NOW. BUT NOW THAT WE HAVE THIS LITTLE UNDERSTANDING, DIG THIS PART RIGHT HERE, CHIEF:

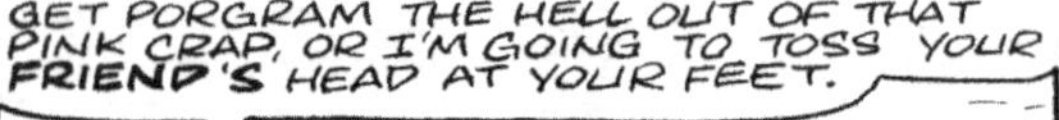
GET PORGRAM THE HELL OUT OF THAT PINK CRAP, OR I'M GOING TO TOSS YOUR **FRIEND'S** HEAD AT YOUR FEET.

GOT **THAT**?

ATTA BOY!
THERE'S A GOOD SANDWICH!
SSSSSSSS

PORGRAM GET OVER THERE AND TIE UP BENKOM.
OKAY.

YOU'RE NOT GOING TO KILL THEM, BOSS?

I WAS. BUT THERE'S A LOT OF POWER IN THIS ROOM. A WHOLE LOT OF POTENTIAL.

NOW THAT I'VE ACCOMPLISHED MY REVENGE...
...NOW WHAT? WHAT'S MY NEXT MOVE?
SNRK
58

THAT DRAGON AZORATAIN ASKED ME IF I WAS GOING TO START A WAR. MAYBE I SHOULD, Y'KNOW?
I NEED TO THINK.

MEANWHILE, IN THE DRAGON LANDS...
NECTAR, PLEASE.
AH! AZORATAIN!

I HEARD YOU WERE IN PRISON FINALLY...

...THE ELDERS HAVING GROWN FED UP WITH ABOUT ONE TRICK TOO MANY!

I DIDN'T EXPECT TO SEE YOU AGAIN FOR ANOTHER ONE HUNDRED MILLENNIA!

NOW, NOW KRASTANE! IF THAT WERE TRUE, WOULD I BE HERE PATRONIZING YOUR FAIR ESTABLISHMENT?

BAH! YOUR SLIME IS WELL KNOWN, TRICKSTER! DON'T ATTEMPT TO--?
WHAT IS IT?
59

MY NAME CHIMES SOMEWHERE IN THE HUMAN CAMPS. I CANNOT ALLOW THIS TO GO UNINVESTIGATED.

IF YOU WILL EXCUSE ME?
HEAR NOW! TAKE YOUR TOMFOOLERY OUTSIDE! I WON'T HAVE--!

Z
CLANG!

SHOW ME... **WHO** UTTERS MY NAME?

WHY, IT IS THE LEADER OF THE STINKY TRIO!

I'M SURPRISED HE COULD **PRONOUNCE** IT LET ALONE REMEMBER IT.

WHAT IS **THIS**?! THE GREAT AXE?! CAN IT BE THAT THIS DOLTISH CREATURE ACTUALLY PASSED THE FAERIE TRIALS?
60

I AM IMPRESSED DESPITE MYSELF. THERE SEEMS TO BE MORE TO THIS NASHERAN THAN WHAT MEETS THE NOSTRILS.
BE THAT AS IT MAY, I CANNOT PASS UP SUCH A WONDERFUL OPPORTUNITY.
OBVIOUSLY THIS CREATURE CANNOT USE THE TALISMAN TO ITS FULLEST POTENTIAL TO BE A THREAT TO ONE SUCH AS I!
SO I WILL TAKE IT FROM HIM. IT IS ONLY RIGHT IN THE SCHEME OF THINGS AFTER ALL. SHOULD A WEE BABE BE ALLOWED TO PLAY WITH A SWORD?
ABSURD!
THE GREAT WEAPON OF FAERIE, WILL SOON BE MINE!
61

HUNH?

SNRK

TURNS OUT BENKOM WAS RIGHT. MAGICK IS THE WAY TO GO IF I WANT TO BE A **REAL** POWER PLAYER.

BUT THIS THING PROBABLY WON'T BE ENOUGH. I'LL NEED **MORE** POWER! ANOTHER TALISMAN IS OUT OF THE QUESTION THOUGH.

AND SO IS LEARNING IT. NASHERANS SUCK AT MAGICK.
WITH ALL OF BENKOM'S BRAGGING, HE'S PROBABLY THE LAMEST MAGICIAN IN THE WORLD.
SO YOU'RE MY REPLACEMENT, HUH?
SHUT UP.

HE'S PRETTY CONFIDENT THAT HIS LITTLE CRAP CAN MAKE HIM KING, THOUGH.
IF HE CAN BEAT THE KING THEN I SURE AS HELL CAN. BUT WHERE CAN I GET MORE MAGICK?
6

BINGO.

HEY! STOP!
OH NO!

LET HIM GO!!
SHUT UP.
LISTEN, YOU TWO.

KEEP AN EYE ON BENKOM AND THE KID. I'LL BE BACK.

CLICK!

DO YOU THINK HE'S GOING TO EAT IT?
63

THAT WOULD BE SERIOUSLY SELFISH AND MESSED UP.

AND WHAT THE HECK WOULD YOUR STUPID BUTTS DO ABOUT IT?

RIGHT.
NOTHIN'.

THAT'S WHY HE LEFT YOU HERE LIKE THE SIMPLE PUNK YOU ARE.

YEAH, I'M TALKING TO Y--!
SHUT UP!!

YOU SHUT UP, YOU PIECE OF CRAP. IT'S NOT LIKE YOU'RE GONNA DO ANYTHING.

IS IT?
YOU SIMPLE HO.

YARSH!!
CHOMP!

SHAKE! SHAKE! SHAKE!
SHAKE! SHAKE!
64

OOPS!
THANKS, GENIUS!

POW!

ROAR!!
SQUEEE!
SQUEEE!
SQUEEE!

THOOM!!

THASH!

WABAM!
65

KOFF.

TRUCE, MAN.

WHERE DID HE TAKE MORT?

HE PROBABLY WENT TO NASHERA. GO STRAIGHT OUT THROUGH THE TUNNELS AND TAKE A HARD RIGHT.

CLICK
66

SPLOOSH!

67

WHERE DID MAESCUS GO?
WHO? BEAT IT, SQUIRT!

MORT!

MORT!!
SOMEBODY SHUT THAT KID UP!!

I GOT 'EM...

KRAK!

MORT!!

MORT!!

I HAVE SOME MORT FOR YOU, DEARIE. WHATCHA TRADE?
YOU HAVE HIM? LET ME SEE.

GUH!!

CRAZY OLE BAT!!

MORT
69

Y'ALL SEEN MORT?
IT'S IN THERE, PIPSQUEAK.

MORT!!

LOOK! ORDER UP AT THE COUNTER LIKE YOU HAVE SOME SENSE OR I'LL BEAT SOME SENSE IN YOU!

HEY.

HEY!

70

HEY!!
I SEE YA THERE, LI'L BIT...
...BUT IF YA AIN'T GOT NOTHIN' TO TRADE I CAN'T HELP YA.

I'M JUST TRYING TO FIND MORT!

WELL, YES, I'VE GOT PLENTY OF MORT HERE. DUG IT UP FRESH FROM THE HUMAN GRAVES LAST NIGHT.

BUT YA NOT TASTING A LICK OF IT IF YA DON'T GOT NOTHIN' TO TRADE.

YUCK!!
SWAK!

SOMEBODY GET THIS LITTLE BRAT!

C'MERE!
71

KRAK!

BAM!

SHEESH, HE'S STRONG! IS THIS **YOUR** KID, HEDDARK?

BUMP!

HOW ABOUT **THAT**! ANOTHER APE/LIZARD HYBRID!
THEY GIVEN YA A HARD TIME, KID? LET ME GET YOU SOMETHING TO EAT!
!
72

WHERE'D YOU GET THIS AXE, MAESCUS? IT IS MAGICK, RIGHT?

YEAH, I GOT IT OUT OF FAERIE.
IN THE FIRE LANDS.

WHERE'S THAT?

TURNS OUT YOU CAN GET THERE IN THE TUNNELS IF YOU GO FAR ENOUGH WEST.

WHAT ELSE DOES IT DO?

WW, THE GUY SAID SOMETHING ABOUT OT PUTTING IT DOWN OR I'LL HAVE TO UEST FOR THE SECRET NAME AGAIN.

BUT HOW DOES IT--?
KID!!!
SHUT THE FRAG UP OR I'LL BITE YOUR DAMN HEAD OFF!
73

SO YOU AREN'T GOING TO EAT ME?

I WASN'T PLANNING ON IT, BUT--!
WAIT!
SO WHAT IS THIS ABOUT?

IT'S ABOUT POWER, BOY!
NEXT LEVEL STUFF, YOU GET ME?
NASHERA'S ALL ABOUT WHO'S THE STRONGEST... THE MOST POWERFUL!

WITH THIS AXE AND YOUR MAGICK, I'M GOING TO MOVE UP IN THE WORLD!

IN FACT, ALL THE WAY TO THE TOP!

YOU'RE ABOUT TO HELP ME BECOME THE NEXT KING OF NASHERA!
NEXT:
"TEACHER PET"

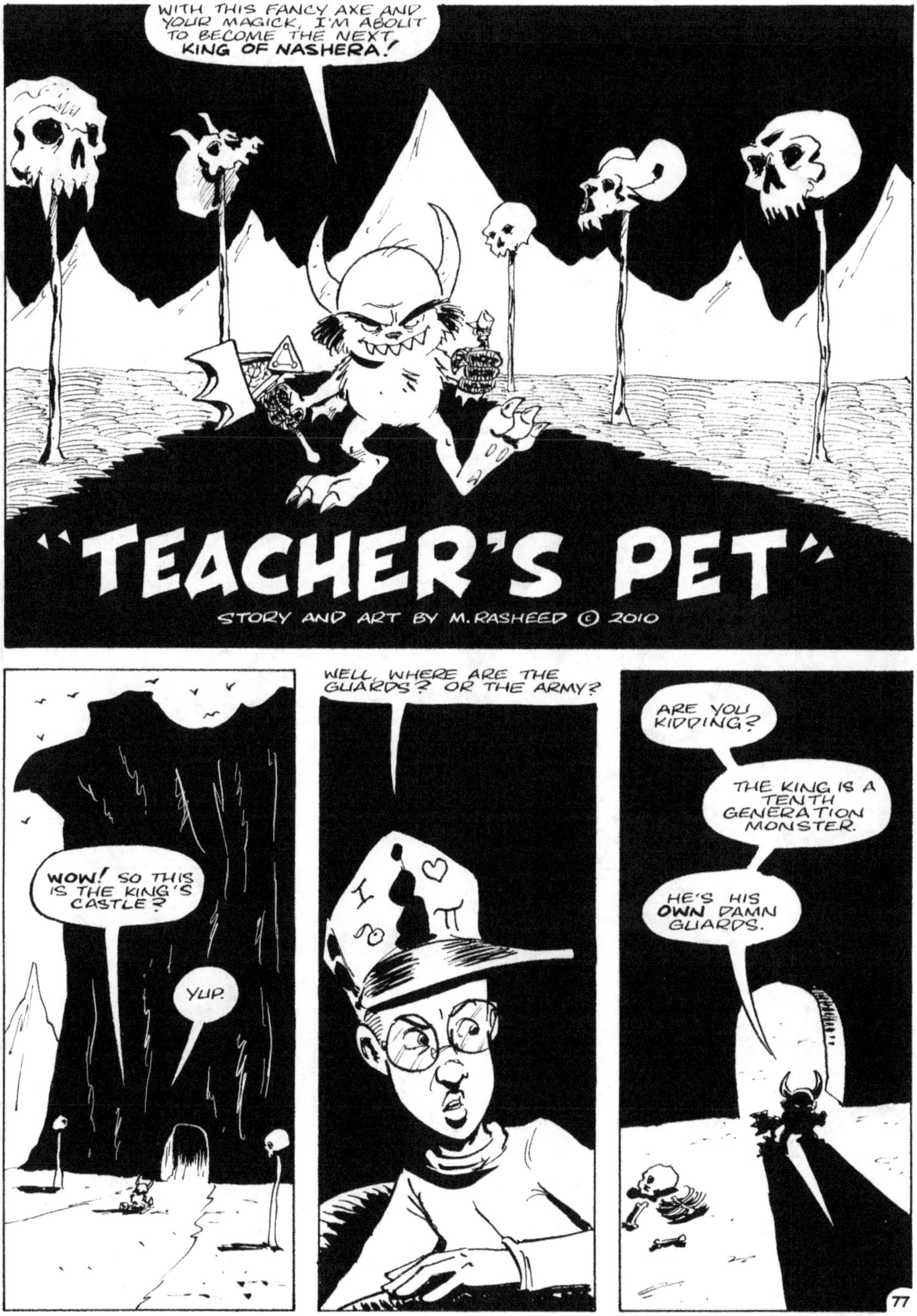

WITH THIS FANCY AXE AND YOUR MAGICK, I'M ABOUT TO BECOME THE NEXT **KING OF NASHERA!**

"TEACHER'S PET"

STORY AND ART BY M. RASHEED © 2010

"TENTH GENERATION?"
WHAT DOES THAT MEAN?

THAT'S JUST NASHERAN CULTURE TALK.

A 'GENERATION' IS TALKIN' ABOUT HOW MANY ANIMALS ARE IN YOU.

I'M A THIRD GENERATION MONSTER, MEANING I HAVE BEAR, BULL AND BAT ANCESTORS.

PORGRAM IS A FIRST GENERATION MONSTER?
RIGHT.
BOTH OF HIS PARENTS WERE PIG MONSTERS.

SO THE KING HAS TEN ANIMALS IN HIM. THAT'S WHAT MAKES HIM KING?

THAT'S WHAT MAKES HIM STRONGER.

ONLY THE MOST POWERFUL NASHERAN GETS TO RULE.
78

THE MORE ANIMALS ARE IN YOU, THE MORE POWERFUL YOU ARE. THAT'S WHY PORGRAM AND LODETH FOLLOW YOU...

'CAUSE I'D BUST THEIR HEADS IF THEY DIDN'T.
SO ONLY TENTH GENERATION OR HIGHER MONSTERS COME HERE TO CHALLENGE THE KING USUALLY?

RIGHT.
FOR THE MOST PART.

YOU'VE NEVER BEEN IN HERE BEFORE?

NO.
I'M TRYING TO...
...FIND THE THRONE ROOM.

SO NORMALLY YOU'D **NEVER** COME IN HERE.

NOPE! I WOULDN'T BE CAUGHT **DEAD** IN HERE IF I DIDN'T HAVE YOU AND THIS AXE. IT WOULD BE SUICIDE!
79

SO HE'S A **LOT** STRONGER THAN YOU.
YEAH.

WITH MORE POWERS.
YUP.

AND A **LOT** BIGGER.
PROBABLY.

AND **SCARIER.**
I GUESS.

MAESCUS, I CAN HEAR YOUR HEART.

SO?! I HAVE A BIG HEART!

YOU'RE... ...SQUEEZING M
TOO TIGHT!
OO! SORRY!

YOU'RE **SURE** YOU CAN TAKE HIM WITH THE AXE?

NOT... **NOT REALLY.** BUT YOU CAN DO THAT FREEZE THING TO HIM, RIGHT?
I **GUESS** SO...

MAESCUS, MAYBE WE SHOULD WORK ON A STRATEGY FIRST?

WHO'S THERE?!?
EEP!
81

WHO CHALLENGES ULAM, KING OF NASHERA?!
82

MEANWHILE...
HEY, ANOTHER APE/LIZARD HYBRID! I'VE NEVER SEEN ANOTHER OF MY KIND!

LOOK AT 'CHA! YOU MUST'VE JUST HATCHED!
UH... YEAH, I'M TRYING TO FIND A FRIEND OF MINE.

WHOA! YOU COULDN'T HAVE JUST HATCHED TALKIN' THAT WELL!

BUT YOU'RE SO LITTLE! HERE, HAVE A SEAT. YOU HUNGRY?
WELL, I...

FEFKER BRING US A BOWL OF MORT OVER HERE!
WHAT? NO! I DON'T...!

THAT KID'S NOT WELCOME HERE, HEDDARK! HE'S ALREADY CAUSED ENOUGH TROUBLE!
TAKE HIM OUTSIDE!
83

YOU FRIGGIN' MAKE ME GO OUTSIDE!!
DUDE!!
WHAT?! WHY YOU--!

TAKE IT EASY, FEFKER!
HE DOESN'T KNOW WHAT HE'S--!

BRAK!

BOOH!!

FRAKT!!

THE HECK--?!
ANYBODY ELSE WANNA MAKE ME GO OUTSIDE?
84

UH... C'MON, KID. LET'S GO FIND YOUR FRIEND.
HUH? OH, OKAY.

WHAT ARE YOU LOOKIN' AT?
I DUNNO.

I THOUGHT YOU WERE A SECOND GENERATION MONSTER LIKE ME.

AS STRONG AS YOU ARE, YOU MIGHT BE AS HIGH AS SIXTH.
YOU THINK SO?

WELL, THE THING IS, I'VE NEVER SEEN A KID OF ANY GENERATION AS STRONG AS YOU ARE.

I RAN INTO AN EIGHTH GENERATION HATCHLING A LONG TIME AGO, BUT EVEN HE WAS ONLY AS STRONG AS ANY OTHER KID.
85

YOU ARE A LITTLE SOMETHIN' **SPECIAL**, I THINK.

I LIKE YOU, KID! I'M GONNA HELP YOU OUT!

TEACH YOU HOW TO BE A NORMAL AND PRODUCTIVE NASHERAN LIKE ME!
OKAY.

FIRST OF ALL YOU NEED SOMETHING TO TRADE FOR FOOD AND STUFF.
LOOK AT THIS...

IT'S A BUNCH OF TOYS, OLD TV GUIDES AND CRAP.

NASHERANS ARE ADDICTED TO TELEVISION, YOU SEE?

"WE PEEK THROUGH HUMAN WINDOWS AND WATCH THEIR SHOWS!"

"WE HAVE OUR OWN FAVORITE PROGRAMS, JUST LIKE THEY DO!"

SO WE COLLECT ALL THE MEMENTOS AND PARAPHERNALIA THAT WE CAN GET OF THE SHOWS WE LIKE BEST!

THEN WE TRADE EACH OTHER FOR FOOD AND STUFF FROM OTHER SHOWS!
I THOUGHT YOU...
...WE...
...ATE HUMAN KIDS.

OH, WE DO! THAT'S OUR FOOD!

WE JUST CAN'T DO IT ALL THE TIME OR THEY'LL GET WISE TO US.

LIVE HUMAN CHILD IS A DELICACY! WE DON'T GET TO EAT IT THAT OFTEN.
SMAK!

WE HAVE TO DIG THEIR CORPSES UP OUT OF THE GRAVES AND EAT THAT MOST OF THE TIME.

B-BUT WHAT ABOUT HERO BARS?
THE CANDY?! YUCK! NO! WE CAN'T EAT THAT! IT'S LIKE EATING PLASTIC!
87

THE HATCHLINGS ARE USUALLY KEPT IN THE PEN AND FED FROM THE TROUGH. BUT I CAN SEE HOW **YOU** COULD'VE ESCAPED FROM IT.
WHAT?!

LITTLE KID MONSTERS ARE KEPT IN A PEN?! WHY?
'CAUSE Y'ALL ARE TOO EXCITABLE.

WE WORK **HARD** TO KEEP OUR EXISTENCE SECRET FROM THE HUMANS.

ALL WE'D **NEED** IS ONE OF YOU SQUIRTS RUNNING OVER THERE MUCKING IT UP FOR EVERYBODY!

BUT **YOU** SEEM MATURE ENOUGH TO HANDLE IT.
JUST DON'T LET 'EM SEE YOU.

SO WHAT'S THIS FRIEND OF YOURS LOOK LIKE ANY WAY?
'BOUT THIS TALL...
...BROWN-SKINNED...
WEARS GLASSES AND A BLUE HAT.

HMMM...
SOUNDS **TASTY**.
WHAT'S HIS NAME?
mort.
88

PREPARE TO BE DETHRONED, ULAM!
NOW IT'S MY TURN TO RULE!
WHAT ARE YOU, A THIRD OR FOURTH GEN? I DON'T HAVE TIME FOR THAT CRAP.

YOU MUST HAVE SOME SERIOUS BALLS ON YOU, GNAT.

I HAVE MORE THAN THAT! DRAGON'S FANG THE FAERIE AXE WILL MAKE ALL THE DIFFERENCE!

WHAT? FROM THE KIDDIE STORIES? YOU SAYIN' THAT'S REAL?!

COME DOWN HERE AND FIND OUT!!

HM.
MAYBE I WILL.
89

OR MAYBE I DON'T NEED TO.
?

YOU LOOK PRETTY SCARED TO DEATH AS IT IS.

MAESCUS, LOOK OUT!!
HUH?

OH, HERE.
WAIT, I MEAN YOU--!
AND YOU BROUGHT ME A SNACK, TOO?!

THANKS!!
KRUK!

AAAAAA!
NO!!
90

BAM!

IT SHRANK!

HEY, YOU! COME UP HERE AND BRING ME THAT!
NO WAY!

I MEAN IT!
DON'T MAKE ME CHASE YOU!!

SIGH

...CRIMINEY...

WHERE YA AT, DAMMIT?!
91

PREPARE TO BE DETHRONED, ULAM!
OH, NOT NOW!!

IT IS MY TURN TO RULE!! TURMAT THE NINTH GENERATION NASHERAN HAS COM TO SMASH YOUR INSIGNIFICANT REIGN.

YEAH, YEAH.

THOOM!
LET'S GET THIS OVER WITH.

I'M BUSY!
POW!

BAM!
BOOM!

BOOM!
BOOM!

THUD!

C'MERE!!

I'M **SICK** OF YOU!
BASH!

KRAK!!
YOU'RE LETTIN' MY SNACK ESCAPE, YOU DING-DONG GALOOT!

BAM!

BRAK!
93

BASH
BASH
BASH
BASH

BASH
BASH
BASH
BASH

ALRIGHT! TIME TO EAT!

COME OUT OF THERE, YOU!

WHERE YOU AT?

I'M NOT PLAYIN' AROUND!

GRRRRR...

I'M IN HERE TALKIN' TO MY DAMN SELF.
94

YOU'RE HOLDIN' OUT ON ME AFTER ALL I'VE TAUGHT YA!
I'M NOT, ALRIGHT!
GET OFF OF IT!

MY FRIEND'S NAME REALLY IS 'MORT!'
YEAH, RIGHT.

SEE THAT'S WHY PEOPLE DON'T LIKE DEALING WITH HATCHLINGS!
AW, HELL!!

YOU'RE TRYING TO MAKE ME HIT--!
HEY! IT'S MORT!

WELL, I'LL BE!
95

FOOD!!
NO!

AH!
LEMME GO!

PAP!
QUIT IT!
PUGG!

PUGROFF! HOW'D **YOU** GET HERE? I WAS COMING TO RESCUE YOU! WHO'S **THIS**?
MY TEACHER.
HUH?

THWAP!

NNGH!!
STOP!!!
YUCK!
96

YOU'RE **SERIOUS**, AREN'T YOU?
YEAH! HE'S MY FRIEND! QUIT TRYING TO EAT HIM!

KID, YOU **CAN'T** HAVE A PET HUMAN CHILD IN NASHERA! PEOPLE WILL **ALWAYS** TRY TO EAT IT!

AND YOU CAN'T WATCH IT **FOREVER**!
"PET?"

LOOK!

THE KING IS OUT. I WONDER WHAT'S--!
TIME TO **GO**!

C'MON, PUGG! LET'S GO!
OKAY.

HE SEES US! HE'S COMING THIS WAY!
RUN!!
97

BRING ME THAT KID!

NEXT:
"MOST
WANTE

"MOST WANTED"
STORY AND ART BY M. RASHEED © 2010
GIVE ME THAT KID! IN THE NAME OF THE KING!
101

POW!

THERE'S A LOT MORE COMING!
WE'VE GOTTA GET YOU OUT OF HERE!

DAD, STOP PLAYING AROUND! LET'S GO!

WHAT ARE YOU DOING, HEDDARK?! THIS IS TREASON!

WAP!!

LEAP!
102

YOUR FRIEND MUST BE DELICIOUS!

STOP!! IN THE NAME OF THE KING!

WAM!

WAK! WAK!
103

THAT'S A PRETTY GOOD TRICK.

OVER HERE!
LET'S GET THEM!

URK!

PAP!

THWAK!

BAM!

THUD!

105

KRAK!

MMMH!!

WBAP!
BAP!
BAP!
BAP!
106

PUGG!
DOWN HERE!

THIS SHOULD DO IT.

WE CAN WAIT HERE A BIT 'TIL THE HEAT'S OFF.

SO WHAT HAVE **YOU** BEEN UP TO?
107

IT WAS CRAZY! MAESCUS TRIED TO TAKE DOWN THE MONSTER KING BUT HE GOT TRICKED! I ESCAPED WITH THE AXE!

HE WAS SERIOUSLY TRYING TO GET ME THOUGH.

WHAT HAPPENED TO YOUR MAGICK?

W-WHAT DO YOU MEAN?
WHY DIDN'T YOU ZAP 'EM?

WELL, I...
I DON'T KNOW.

I WAS...
...SCARED, I GUESS.

AND THAT MEANS YOUR SPELLS DON'T WORK?
NO!
108

THEN WHAT'S GOING ON?

I DON'T KNOW!
MORT, YOU HAVE TO STAY CALM IN A FIGHT.

IF YOU PSYCH YOURSELF OUT, YOU'LL LOSE BEFORE IT EVEN STARTS.

ANYWAY!!
THIS AXE IS FROM THE FAERIE LANDS! WE HAVE TO GO TO GET IT ACTIVATED.

MAESCUS SAID WE CAN GET THERE THROUGH THE TUNNELS!
WHATEVER.

YOU HAVE TO GO WITH ME!
I DON'T HAVE TO DO ANYTHING BUT STAY UGLY AND DIE.
109

PUGROFF!!
SHUT UP! UNLESS YOU WANT THOSE GUYS TO EAT YOU!

I'M NOT SCARED OF THEM! I'LL JUST USE MY MAGICK.
OH, NOW YOU'LL USE YOUR MAGIC HUH?

SHUT UP!!
YOU SHUT UP!

IT DOESN'T SOUND LIKE IT'S YOUR FRIEND ANYMORE.

I CAN TAKE IT OFF YOUR HANDS IF YOU'RE DONE WITH IT.

WHY DON'T **YOU** GO UP THERE AND SEE IF THE COAST IS CLEAR?

MAKE YOURSELF **USEFUL**.
THAT'S WHAT **YOU** CAN DO.

GASP
111

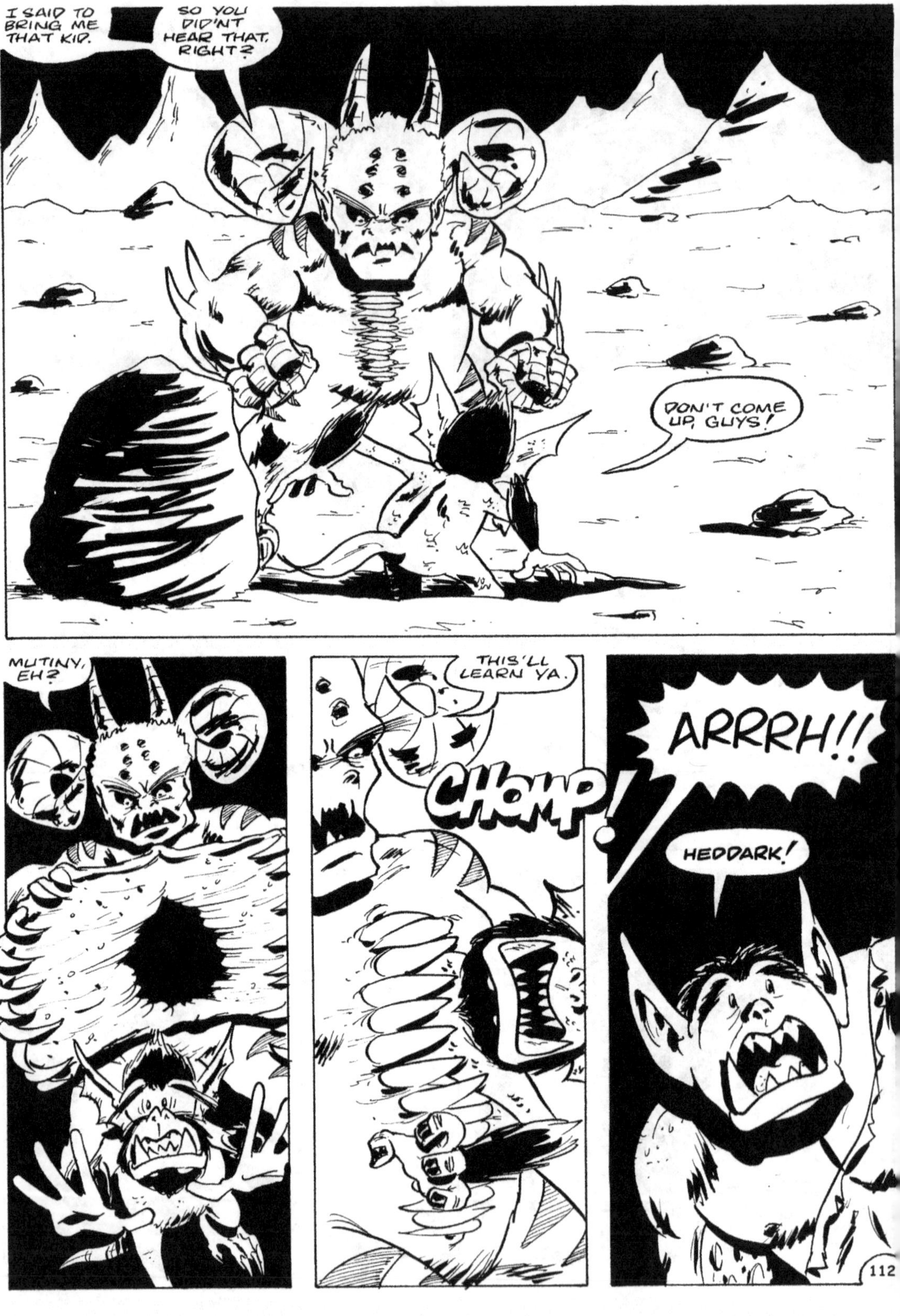

I SAID TO BRING ME THAT KID.
SO YOU DID'NT HEAR THAT, RIGHT?
DON'T COME UP, GUYS!

AH! THERE YOU ARE!
NO!!

I GOT THIS...!

MMH!
HEY!

YOU'RE GOING TO USE YOUR MAGICK NOW WHEN HEDDARK IS STUCK IN HIS CHEST?! ARE YOU CRAZY?!

LET HIM GO!
WHO ARE YOU, PEE WEE?

I'M PUGROFF!
THAT IS MY FRIEND! LET HIM OUT NOW!
113

AND IF I SAY, "NO?"

THEN I'M GOING TO BEAT THE CRAP OUT OF YOU!

NO.

BIFF!

HEH.
YOU'RE TOUGH FOR SUCH A LITTLE TYKE.
UH OH...

SHAKOW!
114

STOMP!!!

YOU'RE GONNA BEAT THE CRAP OUT OF **ME**, HUH?
BASH
BASH
BASH
BASH
BASH
BASH

YOU MEAN LIKE **THIS**, PUNK?!
BASH
BASH
BASH

LIKE THIS?!
BASH
BASH
BASH
BASH
BASH

STOP!!

JUST STOP IT!!
IS THAT WHAT YOU **DO**?! BEAT UP ON LITTLE **KIDS**?!
115

I DON'T MIND.
I REALLY DON'T.

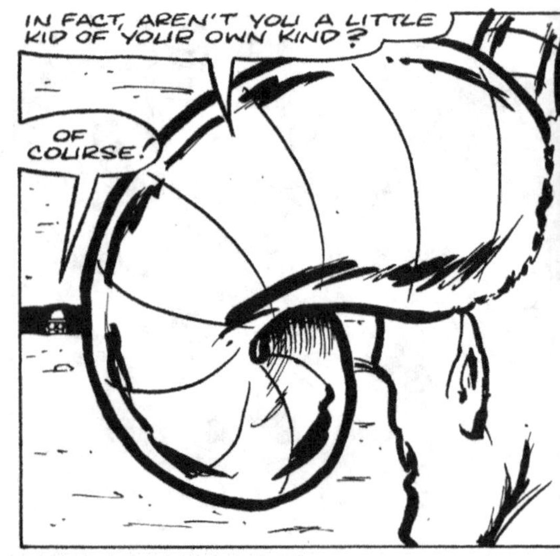
IN FACT, AREN'T YOU A LITTLE KID OF YOUR OWN KIND?
OF COURSE!

WELL, I'M ACTUALLY GOING TO **EAT** YOU.
HOW HARSH IS **THAT**?

NOW ASK ME **AGAIN** IF I GIVE A CRAP ABOUT THRASHING SOME DISRESPECTFU ANKLE-BITER

COME UP OUT OF THERE AN HAND ME THAT AXE
I DON'T HAVE AL DAY.

C'MON.

THAT'S IT.

SIGH

COME HERE.

NOW GIVE IT TO ME.
117

DUNGH!!
BLAMMO!

UK!
WHA--?
WHAT THE HELL?

SLAMMO!

KH...!

CAN YOU FREE YOURSELF, HEDDARK?

NO...,
NO, I'M STUCK.
HE'S GOING TO THROW ME IN THE DUNGEON.
119

PUGROFF AND I WILL RESCUE YOU. I PROMISE. DON'T WORRY, OKAY?

RRRRH...
LITTLE BRAT...

BLAMMO!!

THOOM!!

PUGG!
PUGG!
120

HEY! WAKE UP! YOU'RE ALRIGHT! YOU'RE **TOUGH**!

WH--**WHA**--?
PUGG!

PUGG, WE **HAVE** TO GO TO THE FAERIE LANDS.

WE HAVE TO GO ACTIVATE MY AXE. IT'S THE **ONLY** WAY WE'LL HAVE A REAL SHOT AT DEFEATING THE KING.

SO WE CAN RESCUE YOUR **TEACHER**.
RUB
RUB

HE'S IN BAD SHAPE RIGHT NOW. WE DON'T HAVE A LOT OF TIME.
121

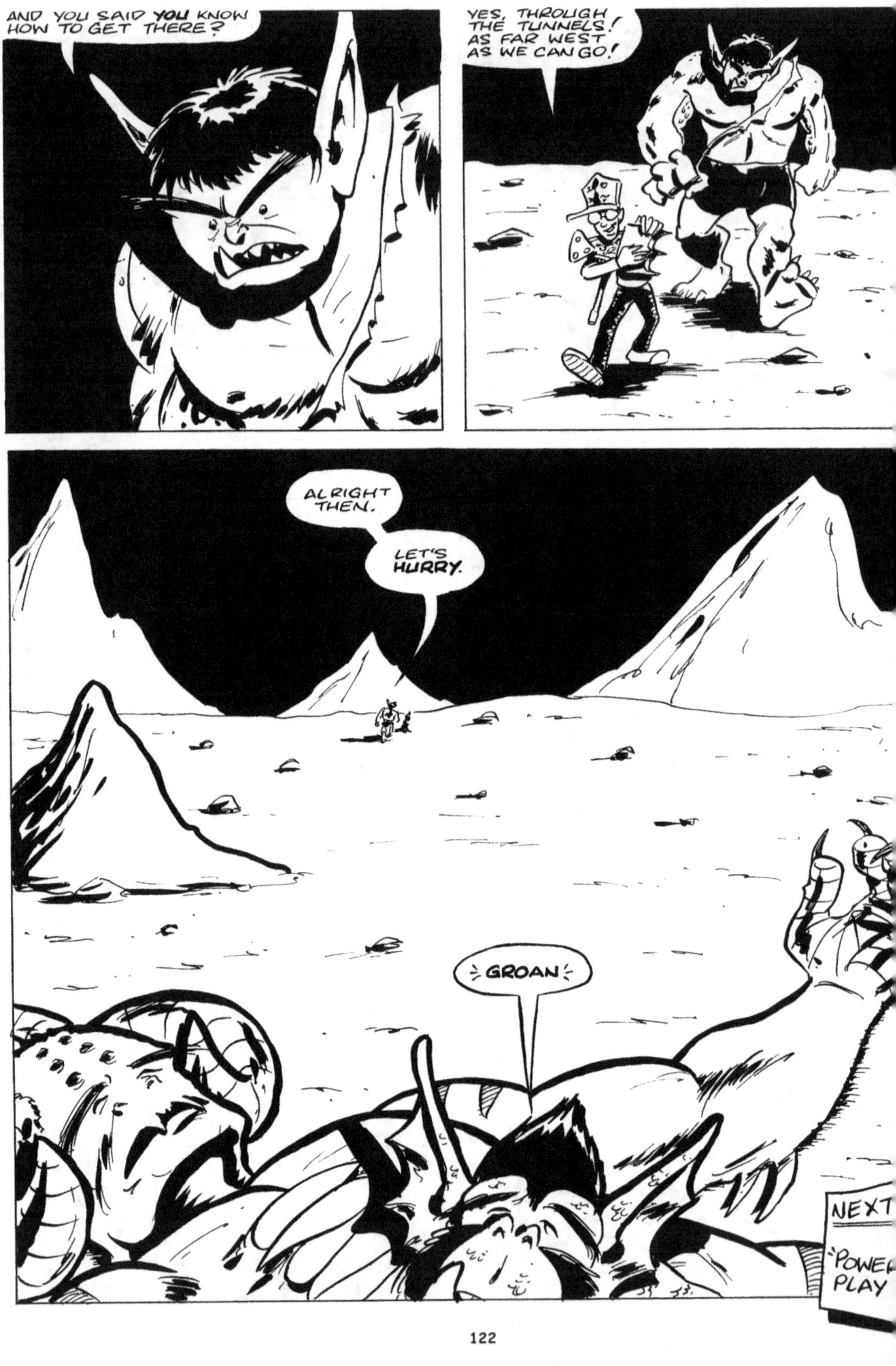

ALRIGHT THEN.

LET'S **HURRY**.

GROAN

NEXT

PLAY

"POWER PLAY"

STORY AND ART BY M. RASHEED© 2010

I MAKE STUFF HAPPEN! I WOULDA FOUND A WAY!
I DON'T LET FEAR KEEP ME FROM DOING CRAP I NEED!

I AM NOT YOU!!

well, i'm glad i'm not YOU!

WHAT DID YOU SAY?!

I THOUGHT NOT.

WE PROBABLY SHOULDA CAME OUT AT THAT LAST DOOR.

NOOO... WE'RE OBVIOUSLY CLOSER TO IT NOW BECAUSE IT'S GETTING A LOT WARMER.

I DON'T FEEL ANYTHING.
TRUST ME, IT'S GETTING WARMER.
127

MAESCUS CALLED IT "THE FIRE LANDS" FOR A REASON.

UHH.
HOT.

THERE'S A DOOR!

IT'S MADE OF METAL.

NOW I'M STARTING TO FEEL IT.

YOU ALRIGHT?
DUDE...

I DON'T THINK I CAN DO THIS.

HOLD ON... JUST LET ME OPEN THIS.

WHOA!
VVOOSH!!

GUH!!

IT'S CLEAR ON THE OTHER SIDE!

TAKE A DEEP BREATH, MORT.

129

ALRIGHT?
IT'S BETTER.

BUT IT'S STILL REALLY HOT THOUGH.

SO WHERE TO FROM HERE?
LOOK!

"THAT JUST HAS TO BE IT."
130

UGH! SHOULD HAVE BROUGHT SOME WATER.
HERE...

THIS WILL GET US THERE FASTER.
THANKS, PUGROFF.

I HOPE THE AIR CONDITIONER IS ON IN THERE.

HALT! WHAT IS YOUR BUSINESS HERE?
131

LET US PASS! WE HAVE COME TO ACTIVATE THE MAGICK AXE OF FAERIE!

YOU ARE A MAGICIAN, HUMAN?
I AM.

THEN YOU MAY ENTER.

ALREADY?!
DRAGON'S FANG HAS ONLY JUST DEPARTED!

DESPITE SOME MINOR FEATS OF ACCOMPLISHMENT, THE NASHERANS HAVE PROVED TRUE TO THEIR BUMBLING REPUTATIONS.

HOW DO YOU KNOW THAT I'M NOT A NASHERAN MONSTER?
THERE IS NOTHING IN YOUR AURA TO SUGGEST SUCH A COMPARISON.
DO YOU CLAIM TO BE?
YES.
132

STRANGE. ALTHOUGH PUNGENT, YOUR ODOR IS **HARDLY** THE RANK ANIMAL MUSK AND ROTTEN CARRION STENCH THE NASHERAN RACE EXHUMES.

DESPITE YOUR VERY HUMAN SPEAK AND MANNERISMS, YOU HAVE AN AURA THAT IS **DEFINITELY** OTHERWORLDLY.
PUGROFF IS ONLY A **CHILD** NASHERAN AND IS STILL ON MILK.

THIS MAY ACCOUNT FOR THE DISCREPANCY.
IT **DOES.** BODY ODORS EMANATE FROM THE FOODS CONSUMED.

THOUGH I AM SURPRISED THAT A HUMAN CHILD WOULD WILLINGLY CHOOSE SUCH A CREATURE AS A COMPANION.

WE HAVE SAVED EACH OTHERS' LIVES NUMEROUS TIMES OVER MANY ADVENTURES.

IT WAS EASIER TO SIMPLY BECOME FRIENDS THAN KEEP TRACK OF THE CUMBERSOME RECORD OF BLOOD DEBTS.
JUST SO.
133

WHO ARE YOU?
I AM PRENT LIGGEN. GUARDIAN OF THE MIGHTY TALISMAN THAT YOU CLUTCH SO TIGHTLY.

ALTHOUGH YOU ARE **ONLY** A HUMAN CHILD AND NOT OF PROUD FAERIE STOCK, I APPROVE OF YOUR CIVILIZED MANNER. A **WELCOME** CHANGE FROM THE UNCOUTH FOOLISHNESS OF THE PREVIOUS, MOST RECENT CHALLENGERS.

I WILL WAIVE CERTAIN CEREMONIAL REQUIREMENTS AND ALLOW YOU TO SPEED ALONG TO YOUR TASK.

BEHIND THIS DOOR AWAITS THE MANIFESTED REALITY OF YOUR GREATEST FEAR. DEFEAT IT AND THE SECRET OF DRAGON'S FANG WILL BE YOURS.
LOOK AT THE DOOR!

IT'S SHRINKING!
13

WHAT DO YOU FEAR, SEEKERS-OF-THE-NAME?
WHAT DO YOU FEAR, FOR THAT IS WHAT YOU MUST FACE...

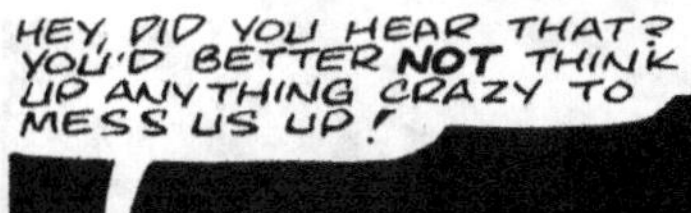

HI, SQUIRT.
MISS ME?

OH, **LOOK**! IT'S THE PUGROFF CLASSIC EDITION!
GIMME YOUR MILK MONEY OR I'LL BUST YOU UP.

I **LOVE** THIS GUY!

PUGROFF, YOU DON'T UNDERSTAND...
THAT'S **NOT** YOU.

IT'S THE PUGG OF MY NIGHTMARES!
WHAT?

AH!!
WHERE'S MY MONEY, PUNK?
136

LET GO!!
RIP!

THAT LITTLE THING IS CRAZY!
DON'T MAKE ME ASK FOR IT AGAIN.

YOU'D BETTER GET OVER THERE AND ZAP'EM!
HUH?!

IT'S YOUR AXE! IF YOU WANT IT TURNED ON YOU HAVE TO BEAT HIM!

AREN'T YOU FORGETTING TO BRING ME SOMETHING TODAY?
137

MY... MILK MONEY? BUT I DIDN'T BRING ANY MONEY WITH ME TODAY, BECAUSE I DIDN'T GO TO SCHOOL!

WHY ARE YOU ALWAYS TRYING TO PISS ME OFF, MORT?

I'M NOT! IF I WOULD HAVE KNOWN THEN I--!

HEY, STOP FREAKING TALKING TO HIM AND ZAP 'EM!
FLINCH!
HUH?

DON'T YOU TURN AWAY FROM ME, FOUR-EYES.
THUD!

YOU GIVE ME YOUR UNDIVIDED ATTENTION, YOU HEAR ME?!
PMBT!
138

AWW, HELL--!

QUIT PICKIN' ON HIM.
WHY DON'T YOU FISH MY MILK MONEY OUT OF THEM TIGHTASS POCKETS AND MIND YOUR OWN DAMN BUSINESS?

HE IS MY BUSINESS, SHRIMP. I SAID "BACK OFF!"
OH, YEAH?

I SAID GET THE FRAG!! OUT OF MY FACE!!
SWISH!

KLUMP!

139

HEY!

WE'RE NOT THROUGH YET.

OH, YES WE **ARE**.

BLLORGH!!

AAAAAA!!

HM.

INTERESTING.
I CERTAINLY HOPE THIS IS NO INDICATION OF WHAT THE FUTURE AGE WILL BE LIKE.

THERE SHOULD BE A WORD CHIMING OVER AND OVER IN YOUR MIND. WHISPER IT INTO THE POMMEL.

THE POWER OF DRAGON'S FANG IS NOW YOURS.

AND IT WILL REMAIN SO UNTIL THE MOMENT YOU SET IT DOWN OR GIVE IT TO SOMEONE.
THEN YOU MUST BRING IT BACK HERE AGAIN.

PLEASURE DOIN' BUSINESS WIT'CHA.
QUITE.
141

WHAT DO YOU MEAN YOU'RE NOT GOING TO GIVE IT TO ME?
I'M NOT. I WON IT FAIR AND SQUARE.
BUT IT'S MINE!
IT USED TO BE.

GIVE IT TO ME!
NO.
YOU DON'T EVEN LIKE MAGICK!
I LIKE THIS.

OTHER THAN THE FACT THAT IT'S A MAGICK... UH... THING...
TALISMAN!!
YEAH. WHY DO YOU NEED IT?

I NEED IT TO FIGHT WITH!
142

YOU DIDN'T FIGHT WITH IT BACK THERE.
IT WASN'T TURNED **ON**!
OH, COME ON. IT'S **STILL** A WEAPON. YOU DIDN'T EVEN **TRY**.

YOU HAD **SPELLS** TO FIGHT WITH AND YOU DIDN'T EVEN TRY. ALL YOU HAD TO DO WAS **TALK** AT HIM!

I'M NOT GIVING YOU ANYTHING SO YOU MIGHT AS WELL STOP THINKING ABOUT IT.
I HATE YOU!

NO, YOU DON'T. YOU HATE **THAT** GUY. AND HE'S GONE NOW.

THE AXE IS MINE SO GET OVER IT.
CONCENTRATE ON YOUR MAGICK.

HEY, ULAM!! WHERE'S MY FRIEND AT?!
!
HE'S DOWN THERE. DON'T STEP ON THAT PART.
143

WELL, WELL, WELL! LOOK, WHO CAME TO VISIT ME!

ARE YOU TOO SCARED NOW?
NO!

WELL, HERE'S YOUR SHOT, CHAMP! DO YOUR THING!

AH!! WHAT THE HECK?!

DID YOU KILL HIM?
NO, THAT WAS THE FAR-FLUNG REMOTE INVEST-MENT.

IT SENT HIM TO THE OTHER SIDE OF THE PLANET.
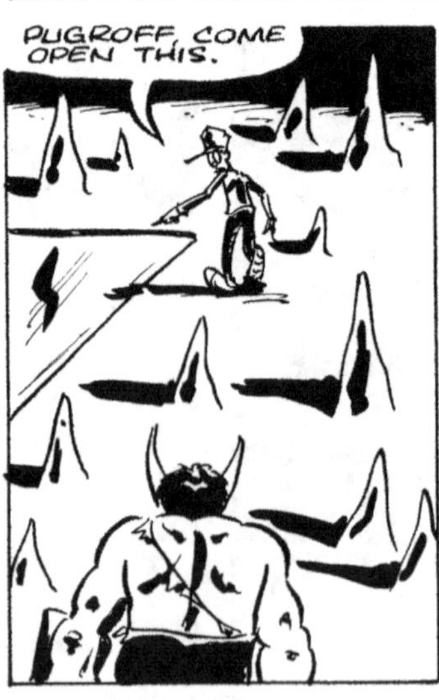
PUGROFF, COME OPEN THIS.

SKRUNK!!
HEDDARK!
144

HEDDARK ARE YOU ALRIGHT?
NOOO...

MAESCUS...?
HELP...
ME...

WE'LL GET YOU BOTH OUT!
"BOTH?"

SHUT UP, I'M DOING IT! LOWER ME DOWN THERE!

AWW, MAN...!
I CAN'T BELIEVE YOU GUYS ARE STILL ALIVE...
...YUCK...!
HERE, HOLD ON...
145

UH... THANKS, FELLAS.

NOTHING MAKES YOU FEEL **MORE** LIKE CRAP THAN BEING SAVED BY PEOPLE YOU TRIED TO KILL.

BUT YOU DON'T HAVE TO WORRY ABOUT THAT ANY MORE. IF YOU NEED ANY-THING AT **ALL**, JUST LET ME AND THE CREW KNOW.

AND **THAT'S** A PROMISE!
END

ABOUT THE AUTHOR

M. Rasheed is a permanent vendor at the North Carolina State Fairgrounds and popularly known for his Cartoon Portraits, which enable lucky patrons to pose with their favorite cartoon characters and celebrities in the artist's fun/friendly drawing style.

Highly prolific, M. Rasheed is also the cartoonist behind the *Monsters 101* graphic novel series, *Wild Hunt*, and many fascinating web stories, which includes a YouTube channel featuring original Adobe Flash animated shorts.

He received his B.F.A. from the College of Creative Studies in Detroit, Michigan and is proud to admit that he was one of the "Dogs of 1-D" from the Joe Kubert School of Cartoon and Graphic Art, Inc.

Additional copies of this book
and other titles from
Second Sight Graphix
are available for ordering
at www.mrasheed.com,
at www.amazon.com,
and at your local book store.
You may also use the
handy coupon on the
following page to order
by mail.

For more info about
our titles please
visit our Web site!

http://www.mrasheed.com

So, you would like to be one of the Shemesu Heru, the Followers of Second Sight? Then you'd better start collecting more books from Second Sight Graphix! Here's a few more titles you'll enjoy:

_____**How to Create a Comic Book and Get Rich Doing it**..$10.00

_____Monsters 101, book five
"Monsters and Monarchy"..$15.00

_____Monsters 101, book three
"Devil Take the Hindmost"...$15.00

_____Monsters 101, book two
"Heroes and Devils"...$15.00

_____Monsters 101, book one
"From Bully to Monster"...$15.00

_____**Releasing the Cartoonist Within**..$12.00

Second Sight Graphix, Dept OPS
7413 Six Forks Road, Suite 203 Raleigh, NC 27615-4190

Please send me the books I have checked above. I am enclosing $_______________________
I am adding $4.50 for the first book and $1.00 for each additional book to cover postage and handling. Send check or money orders only. No CODs. Do not send cash. Please allow up to six weeks for delivery.

NAME____

ADDRESS____

CITY______________**STATE**________**ZIP**______________

www.ingramcontent.com/pod-product-compliance
Lightning Source LLC
LaVergne TN
LVHW050536100826
845148LV00002B/580

* 9 7 8 0 5 7 8 0 5 6 3 6 4 *